Nat did it

Written by Sarah Rice

Illustrated by Dan Lewis

Collins

Nat tips it.

Nat pats it.

Nat tips it.

Nat sips it.

Sam taps it.

Sam dips it.

Sam taps it.

Sam sips it.

Nat naps in it.

Nat tips it.

Nat naps in it.

Nat did it.

After reading

Letters and Sounds: Phase 2

Word count: 38

Focus phonemes: /s/ /a/ /t/ /p/ /i/ /n/ /m/ /d/

Curriculum links: Understanding the World

Early learning goals: Reading: read and understand simple sentences, use phonic knowledge to decode regular words and read them aloud accurately

Developing fluency

- Your child may enjoy hearing you read the book.
- You could each choose one character (Nat or Sam) and then read the pages that are about that character.

Phonic practice

- Say the word **dips** on page 7. Ask your child if they can sound out each of the letter sounds in the word **dips** d/i/p/s and then blend them.
- Now ask them to do the same with the following words:

  taps   sips   naps

- Look at the "I spy sounds" pages (14 to 15) together. How many words can your child point out that contain the /i/ sound? (e.g. *igloo, vinegar, biscuit, picture, ink, insect, Italy*)

Extending vocabulary

- Look at the pictures of Nat. Talk about what she is doing in each picture. (*pouring ketchup and spilling it, pouring tea and spilling it, falling asleep and knocking over her drink*)
- Now do the same with the pictures of Sam. (*dipping a vegetable stick in mayonnaise, sipping her tea*)
- Ask your child to think of words to describe what Nat is doing and what Sam is doing. Can your child point out how they are different or similar? (*Nat is messy. Sam is tidy.*)